Disney's
THE
LION KING

ADVANCE
PUBLISHERS

Published by Advance Publishers, L.C.
Maitland, FL 32751 USA
www.advancepublishers.com
Produced by Judy O Productions, Inc.
Designed by SunDried Penguin
© 2006 Disney Enterprises, Inc.
Lion King
Printed in the United States of America

The Lion King Mufasa and Queen Sarabi had a cub they named Simba. On the day of his presentation, Rafiki the baboon introduced Simba to all the animals of Pride Rock. Only Scar, Mufasa's brother, didn't attend the ceremony. He was angry because Simba's birth meant he would never have the chance to be king.

Simba grew into a happy little cub. One day, his father told him he would be the next king and Simba proudly told his Uncle Scar the good news. He said he would rule all of the Pride Lands, except for the shadowy place in the distance. "Dad says I'm not allowed to go there," Simba said. "And he's absolutely right, Simba," agreed Scar, slyly. "Only the bravest lions can go to the elephant graveyard." When Simba heard that, he raced home and convinced his friend, Nala, to go with him to explore.

Zazu, Mufasa's advisor, tried to stop Simba and Nala, but they managed to run away from him. When they got to the graveyard, the three of them were cornered by the hyenas, Bonzai, Shenzi and Ed, sent by Scar to kill the lion cubs. But just as the hyenas were about to pounce, Mufasa leapt to the cubs' rescue and frightened the hyenas away.

Mufasa was very angry and sent Nala home with Zazu. Then he and Simba went for a walk. Simba asked Mufasa if they would always be together and Mufasa told him to look up at the stars. "Those are the great kings of the past looking down on us," he said. "Those kings will always be there to guide you, and so will I."

Meanwhile, Scar made a plan with the hyenas to get rid of Mufasa and Simba forever. Scar led Simba to a gorge and told him to wait there for his father, who had a wonderful surprise for him.
Then Scar signalled the hyenas who started a stampede of wildebeest – straight towards Simba! He clung to a tree branch and as he was just about to fall, Mufasa appeared and carried him to safety.

But Mufasa slipped from the ledge and fell. As he struggled back up the cliff face, Scar appeared and dug his claws into Mufasa. "Long live the king!" he sneered before pushing Mufasa off the cliff to his death.

When Simba found his father's lifeless body, he thought it was his fault. Scar arrived and said, "Run away, Simba! Run away and never return." Simba fled, pursued by the hyenas till he was alone in the desert. Scar returned to Pride Rock with the news of the deaths of Mufasa and Simba, and announced himself as the new king.

Simba wandered the desert until he
collapsed from heat and exhaustion.
He was found by the meerkat, Timon,
and the warthog, Pumbaa, who took
him with them to the jungle to live their
"Hakuna Matata" life – which means
"no worries"! As Simba grew up,
he learned to like his new life, and
tried to put the past behind him.

One day, the lioness Nala arrived, searching for help. When she realized that she'd found Simba, she was very happy. Nala told Simba how Scar and the hyenas had destroyed the Pride Lands under their evil and greedy rule. She asked Simba to return with her to take his place as king, but Simba told Nala he couldn't and ran off.

Wandering alone, Simba met the baboon, Rafiki, who told him he knew his father. "My father is dead," said Simba, angrily. But Rafiki said, "He's alive, I'll show you!" He led Simba to a pool of water and showed him his own reflection. "You see, he lives in you!" explained Rafiki. Then Simba heard his father's voice calling to him to return to Pride Rock. As Simba raced home, Rafiki found Nala, Timon and Pumbaa and told them, "The king has returned!"

When he got to Pride Rock, Simba realized his friends had followed him. They devised a plan and Simba confronted Scar, who finally admitted to killing Mufasa and blamed the hyenas for everything. When Scar refused to leave, Simba and Scar fought, and Scar fell from the rock into a den of angry hyenas, never to be heard of again. As the rain washed away the destruction of Scar's reign, Simba climbed Pride Rock to take his rightful place as king.

Some months later, the animals of the Pride Lands gathered at Pride Rock to welcome the son of King Simba and Queen Nala. When Rafiki held the new lion cub high, all the animals knew that the circle of life would continue, unbroken, forever.

The End